YOUNG INDIANA JONES™

and the

TOMB OF TERROR

Les Martin

FANTAIL

FANTAIL PUBLISHING
AN IMPRINT OF PUFFIN ENTERPRISES

Published by the Penguin Group
27 Wrights Lane, London w8 5tz, England.
Penguin Books Australia Ltd., Ringwood, Victoria, Australia.
Penguin Books (NZ) Ltd., 182–190 Wairau Road, Auckland 10, New Zealand.
Penguin Books Ltd., Registered Offices: Harmondsworth, Middlesex, England.

First published in the UK by Fantail Publishing, 1990
Young Indy novels are conceived and produced by Random House Inc.,
in conjunction with Lucasfilm Ltd.

1 3 5 7 9 10 8 6 4 2

0140902155

Printed by Clays Ltd, St Ives plc

Miss Loader

YOUNG
INDIANA JONES™

Chapter
1

'I'm not sure I should let you go off to see the Pyramids on your own, Junior,' Marcus Brody told Young Indiana Jones.

'Do me a favour. Don't call me *Junior*.' Indy gave a grimace. 'My dad calls me *Junior*. I call myself *Indiana* – Indy, for short.'

'I'm not sure your father would approve,' said Marcus.

'Dad isn't around now,' Indy was quick to reply. 'What he doesn't know, won't hurt him.'

'Your father may be far away, but he's still my closest friend,' said Marcus. 'I promised to keep a close eye on you. He warned me about you. He said you are, er, a bit too adventurous.'

'Sure he didn't say foolhardy?' Indy said with a grin. 'That's what he tells me.'

'Perhaps he did,' Marcus admitted. 'In any case, it doesn't matter. Your safety is my responsibility.'

'There's nothing dangerous about going to see the Pyramids,' Indy protested. 'All tourists go to see the Pyramids. You must be the first who hasn't.'

'I'm not in Egypt as a tourist,' said Marcus self-importantly. 'I'm here to make purchases for my museum. There are some people I must see in Cairo and there's only one day left to do it in. We sail up the Nile to Luxor tomorrow.'

'That's why I have to see the Pyramids today,' Indy said triumphantly. 'I mean, that's why I'm in Egypt. Right? To see the famous sights. To widen my background in history.'

Indy knew that Marcus couldn't argue with that. Learning about ancient history was the official reason for Indy's coming to Egypt during his summer vacation.

Of course, that wasn't the real reason. The real reason was that Indy's dad, Professor Henry Jones, was writing a major historical paper. He didn't want Indy hanging around the house getting under his feet. When the Professor learned that his old college chum, Marcus Brody, was going to Egypt on an archaeological shopping trip, he persuaded Marcus that it would do wonders for Indy's education if the boy went with him.

Indy thought it was a miracle they had made it this far. Marcus had almost taken a train to

6

California rather than to New York. He had written down the wrong date for the departure of their liner to England and he had misplaced their tickets for the ship that was to take them to Egypt on its way to India through the Suez Canal.

Marcus was very much at home in the museum where he was assistant curator, but in the outside world, where nothing was labelled and put in glass cases, Marcus had an uncanny knack of getting lost anywhere, any time.

Fortunately Indy had been around to get them on the right train, and double-check their sailing date to England. He even found the missing boat tickets. Marcus had put them in a book for safekeeping. Now Indy struggled to keep a straight face as Marcus gave him directions to the Pyramids.

'There'd be no problem if I were going with you,' Marcus said. 'But since I'm not, you'll have to go to the hotel desk. I'm sure they have some excellent group tours that aren't too expensive. He handed Indy a British gold sovereign. 'Here, this ought to more than cover it. It's worth over five American dollars. You can keep the change for pocket money.'

Indy thanked him, then asked, 'Don't the Egyptians have any currency of their own?'

'They do, but English money is accepted just as easily,' Marcus told him. 'Egypt is a British protectorate.'

'Protectorate?' wondered Indy. 'What's England protecting Egypt from?'

'England isn't that much interested in protecting Egypt,' said Marcus. 'But they are *very* interested in protecting the Suez Canal here. The Canal is the lifeline of the British Empire. It gives them a direct shipping lane to their colonies in the Far East — India, Burma, Malaya, Hong Kong. That's why they took over Egypt.'

'So that's why I saw so many British soldiers in the streets,' said Indy. 'Is the Canal near here?'

'About seventy miles from Cairo,' Marcus said. 'But the British have troops all over Egypt. They don't want anyone getting any ideas about fighting for control of the Canal.'

'Who would want to?' asked Indy.

Marcus smiled. 'Nobody, really. The idea of war is unthinkable in these modern days. But the big European powers have old-fashioned fears of each other. The British, for instance, worry about the German Kaiser. Quite foolish, of course. The Kaiser is quite a progressive ruler. Germany is making great strides forward. The last thing Germany wants is a war.'

As Indy looked at the gold sovereign in his

hand a thought struck him. 'Is our money any good here?' he asked. He was thinking of the twenty-seven dollars in his back pocket. His life-savings, which he had earned by doing everything from weeding gardens to tending sheep.

'It certainly is,' Marcus said. 'I plan to use it to buy some important pieces. If I do, my future at the museum is assured. I'll have a good shot at becoming head curator some day.'

'I'll keep my eyes open when I'm at the Pyramids,' said Indy. 'Maybe I'll spot something good.'

Marcus chuckled. 'No chance of that. Grave robbers have been looting Egyptian tombs for thousands of years. And archaeologists have been digging ever since Napoleon came here over a century ago. That's the trouble with living in 1913. There's so little left to discover.'

'Well, maybe I'll spot some bargains on sale for you,' Indy offered.

Marcus shook his head firmly. 'I have to warn you about that. Don't buy any so-called ancient relics from local merchants. They are all fakes. Total fakes.'

Indy sighed to himself. Marcus always managed to take the fun out of everything. Well, he'd listen to Marcus about the local merchants. He was probably right about that. But there was no way Indy was going on a guided tour of the Pyramids.

Indy had seen one of those guided tours leaving the hotel when he and Marcus arrived. A pack of overweight, overdressed men and women, already complaining of the heat. While they grumbled, a bored guide kept up a constant stream of memorized chatter. That was not the way Indy wanted to see the Pyramids, or anything else. He wanted to see things on his own, with his own eyes.

As for Marcus's worries, they made Indy want to laugh.

But an hour later, in the shadow of the Pyramids, Indy wasn't thinking of laughing any more.

He was thinking of shouting — shouting for dear life.

Chapter 2

The man facing Indy was at least six feet tall. He weighed well over two hundred pounds. A lot of it was fat, but the rest was bulging muscle. His mouth was twisted into a sneer under a big black moustache. His huge hand was clenched in a fist inches from Indy's nose.

'So you want change, Englishman?' he demanded in a snarling voice.

'I'm an American,' Indy corrected him automatically.

'American, English — what is the difference?' the man said. 'You are far from home and alone. Forget about your precious change if you value your worthless life.'

'But we agreed on the fare,' Indy insisted.

'That was *there*,' the man said. 'This is here.'

Indy's heart sank. He realized how right the man was. And how dumb he, Indy, had been. Indy should have seen the cabbie in front of the hotel for what he was — a vulture eager to swoop down on an unwary tourist.

The man had been all smiles when he begged Indy to get into his horsedrawn cab. The price he quoted was very low, but all that was history. When they arrived at the Pyramids, Indy gave the man the gold sovereign. Then he asked for his change.

'This is highway robbery,' Indy protested.

'A robber? You call me a robber?' The man's swarthy face darkened with rage.

'That's the nicest word I can think of,' Indy said. He knew he should watch his step, but he was too angry.

Suddenly the man smiled. A nasty smile. 'If I am a robber, I will be a good one. Empty all your pockets.'

Indy thought of his life savings in his back pocket. Why hadn't he kept his mouth shut? This was his day for dumb moves. The cabbie, on the other hand, had been smart.

They were in a secluded spot, off to one side of the three great Pyramids. Indy's back was against an ancient stone wall. There was no one to hear him call for help, and nowhere he could run. He could kiss his twenty-seven dollars goodbye.

The cabbie's eyes gleamed greedily as Indy

turned his side pockets inside out. The man was annoyed when all he saw were a jackknife, a lucky Indian head penny, a Ute arrowhead, and a badly wrinkled handkerchief.

'Your back pockets, too,' he snarled.

But as Indy reluctantly reached for his cash, another voice ordered, 'Don't.'

A boy about Indy's age but slimmer and considerably shorter had appeared around the corner of the wall. He and the driver argued hotly in Egyptian. Then the angry man threw some coins at Indy's feet. He climbed into the driver's seat of his cab. Giving the horse a mean flick of his whip, he sped off in a cloud of dust.

'Better count your change,' the boy said. 'I'm afraid that guy's not very honest.'

Indy didn't know what surprised him more — that this kid had got rid of the bruiser so easily, or that he spoke perfect English. It didn't add up. The boy had dark skin. He wore a ragged white cotton turban and robes. His dust-covered bare feet were those of an Egyptian street boy.

'Hey, where do you come from?' Indy asked.

'Right here. Cairo, Egypt.'

'Sure it's not Cairo, Illinois?' said Indy. 'That's what you sound like.'

The boy shrugged. 'You're American, so I talk like an American.' Then he changed his accent to say, 'If you were British, my dear chap, I'd talk like this. *Si vous seriez Francais, je parlerais comme ci. Ich kann auch Deutsch sprechen. E Italiano.*'

He grinned at Indy's amazed look. 'We Egyptians are good at languages. We have to be. Almost nobody else speaks Arabic.'

'Speaking of which, what did you say to that guy who was ripping me off?' Indy asked.

'I just mentioned my uncle. He's president of the Cairo cab drivers' association,' said the boy. 'This guy hasn't joined. They can be real rough on an outsider muscling in on their territory, much less giving them all a bad name.'

'Well, lucky for me you showed up when you did.' Indy gave a friendly grin.

'It wasn't exactly luck,' the boy said. 'I saw him pick you up outside your hotel. I heard you say where you were going, so I hitched a ride out here. I figured he'd pull some funny stuff.'

'Gee, you went to all that trouble to help a stranger,' said Indy. He shook his head in wonder. 'Thanks a million.'

'You won't need nearly that much,' the boy said.

'Huh?' said Indy.

'My rates are really very reasonable,' the boy said. 'You can't really see the pyramids without a guide, and I happen to be the best in the business.'

Indy grinned as light dawned on him.

'And what are your rates?' he asked.

'Four shillings English, or a dollar American,' replied the boy.

Indy shrugged. 'Okay.'

'No, no.' The boy was plainly exasperated. 'You say, one shilling.'

'Okay,' said Indy. 'One shilling.'

'Three shillings,' said the boy.

'Two shillings. And not a penny higher!' Indy stood firm.

'It's a deal.' The boy was pleased. 'See, you're learning Egyptian ways already.'

'You're a good teacher,' Indy told him. 'My name's Indiana Jones. Indy, for short. What's yours?'

'Sallah Mohammed Faisel el Kahir,' said the boy. 'Sallah, for short.'

'You know, Sallah,' Indy said, as they shook hands, 'I've got a hunch that this is the beginning of a beautiful friendship.'

Chapter
3

The pyramids were huge. Indy gazed at the three largest, the Great Pyramid of King Cheops, and the two slightly smaller ones of his son and grandson. Beside them were three other very small pyramids, for their queens, and nearby, tombs of their high officials.

'I've read about the pyramids,' said Indy, 'but I had no idea they were so awesome. As awesome as the desert out there.'

Indy looked out over the sea of tan-coloured sand. The dunes were ridged like cresting waves. They stretched to the horizon on one side of the pyramids. Looking in the other direction, he could see fields of wheat and corn. The crops grew on the ribbon of land that ran beside the Nile. It was easy to see how vital the river was and always had been to the country.

Indy was still slightly out of breath, though the hot wind off the desert had already dried the sweat on his skin. Sallah and he had climbed to the top of the Great Pyramid. They had to stretch for handholds and footholds on the large rough granite building blocks.

Sallah told Indy that the Pyramids used to be covered by a layer of polished stone. Arabs and Turks and other conquerors had stripped if off to use in the construction of their own buildings.

'But still the pyramids remain the wonders of the world,' Sallah went on, his voice filled with pride. 'We Egyptians had the greatest civilization in the world, and it lasted for thousands of years.'

'Thousands of years of history — that's hard for an American to imagine,' said Indy. 'Our country just goes back a few hundred years. Unless you count the Indians, which you should. But almost no one does.'

'Your country has a long way to go,' said Sallah. 'Its civilization still has to pass the only true test . . . the test of time.'

'These pyramids have.' Indy gazed at them with admiration. 'The pharaohs really built them to last.'

'They had a good reason to,' Sallah told him. 'These pyramids were their final resting places. It was very important that their remains were not disturbed.'

'Part of their religion, huh?' said Indy.

17

Sallah nodded. 'They believed that each person was born with a spirit twin called a Ka. When a person died, his Ka needed the person's body or picture or statue to live in. Otherwise it had to wander forever homeless. So before a pharoah or a nobleman died, he arranged a safe home for his Ka. He made sure his corpse would be preserved as a mummy. The mummy was then put in a tomb and pictures and statues of himself were laid beside it. There were food, tools, weapons, and anything else his Ka might want. He even had pictures of his servants in his tomb. That way their Kas could serve his.'

'Neat idea,' said Indy. 'So the mummies of the pharoahs are still in there?'

Sallah shook his head, 'There were rebellions and wars. The pyramids were looted. After that, pharoahs stopped putting up pyramids. They hid their tombs in hillsides to give their Kas safer homes.'

'And how did that work out?' Indy asked.

'Not any better,' said Sallah. 'Those tombs were found and looted, too. It's funny in a way. All the gold and jewels that the pharoahs piled up for their Kas turned out to be their ruin.'

'Yeah, I've heard about that,' Indy said. 'I'm in Egypt with Marcus Brody, a friend of my dad's, and he's interested in ancient relics. He says that everything made of gold was melted down over the centuries. Marcus says it's a shame,' said Indy. 'I call it a crime. Nobody has the right to destroy pieces of history. It's like robbing us all of our memory.'

A smile appeared on Sallah's face when he heard this. His dark brown eyes gleamed.

'Then you like ancient relics?' he asked.

Indy had a good idea what was coming. But he kept a straight face when he answered, 'I sure do.'

'Then you will want to buy this,' Sallah said. He slipped his hand into his robe and pulled out an object wrapped in a white cotton rag. He unwrapped it with elaborate care, as if it were immensely precious.

It was a gold ring with a pale green carved stone. 'Very valuable,' said Sallah. 'From the time of the pharoahs, but I like you. We are friends. I will give it to you for only one hundred dollars.'

Indy grinned. 'Sorry, no sale.'

'But it is of the finest quality. The very best,' Sallah declared. 'Here, take a look.'

He pressed the ring into Indy's hand. Indy had no choice but to take it and pretend to examine it.

'Look at that figure carved on the jade stone,'

Sallah had put on his best salesman's voice. 'It is Osiris. The greatest of the gods. The god of birth and death. The ruler of all life.'

Indy decided the joke had gone far enough.

'I hate to be a wet blanket, Sallah,' he said. 'And I know you have to make a living, but you'll have to find another tourist to peddle this to. You see, I know there aren't any ancient treasures to buy nowadays. Any *real* ones, anyway. I know it's a fake.'

Sallah drew himself up indignantly. 'A fake? You think I am a swindler? If I were, I would ask you five dollars. And I'd settle for two. This is absolutely genuine. I swear it to you. On the souls of my ancestors.'

Indy sighed to himself. Sallah had to be a natural-born genius at acting. His performance would have convinced anyone who didn't know better.

Sallah's outrage grew even more convincing. When Indy shook his head and tried to hand Sallah back the ring, Sallah wouldn't take it.

'You haven't really looked at it,' Sallah protested. 'Take a close look. Then try to tell me it is a fake.'

Indy shrugged. He would have to go through the motions before Sallah would give up.

Indy examined the ring. He had to admit that

the gold was of beautiful workmanship, and the jade carving of Osiris was that of a master artist.

Indy looked more closely at the figure of the god. Osiris stood with his arms crossed in front of him. He had a shepherd's crook in one hand, a farmer's wheat flail in the other. He wore a triple crown on his head. His bearded face was turned in profile, with only one eye showing.

Indy looked into that eye . . . and was blinded. Blinded by dazzling light . . . light stronger than the sun in the cloudless Egyptian sky . . . light beamed from the eye of the god.

A moment later, his vision cleared again.

By that time, he was sure of one thing.

It was impossible, but the ring in his hand was real!

Chapter
4

Sallah was smiling. 'You saw it? The eye of Osiris?'

Indy nodded, still stunned.

'Wonderful what the ancients could do,' Sallah said. 'They made that eye of some kind of stone we cannot identify. Maybe a jewel, maybe not. Like a diamond but a thousand times brighter. Amazing, right?'

Indy nodded again. But he was not sure Sallah was right. The light from the ring had seemed too strong to come from anything found on earth. It was ungodly. Or maybe godly. Indy did not know which.

'Now you know the ring is real, you must agree it is dirt cheap at a hundred dollars,' Sallah went on.

'It would be cheap at a thousand,' Indy murmured, staring at the ring.

Sallah sighed. 'Come on, no joking. Let us be

serious. I say a hundred dollars. What do you offer?'

'Nothing,' was Indy's response.

'No, no! That is not the way to bargain,' Sallah patiently explained. 'You have to offer *something*, so I am not insulted. Ten dollars, maybe. Then I say ninety. Then you offer fifteen or twenty. And we go on from there. When in Egypt, you must do like an Egyptian. Now, please, what do you offer?'

'Nothing,' Indy repeated firmly. 'A ring like this is a priceless piece of history. It doesn't belong in private hands. It belongs in a museum, where all people can see it.'

Indy's voice was earnest. 'You are an Egyptian,' he continued. 'You should want it to be in an Egyptian museum. That way your people can see it and be proud. Like when they look at the pyramids here. When you rob the graves of your ancestors, you rob yourselves as well.'

Indy had noted the pride with which Sallah had talked about his country's past. Now he saw he had scored a direct hit on Sallah's conscience.

Sallah hung his head. 'You make me feel ashamed.'

'You should be,' Indy could not keep the anger from his voice. Then he added more gently, 'But not too much. People who buy these treasures are guilty, too. I don't even think the guy I'm with in Egypt, Marcus Brody, should buy things to take out of the country. He says that his museum can show them to more people than the one they've started in Cairo. Still, I don't agree with what he is doing.'

'I wish I could give the ring to that museum, believe me,' said Sallah. 'Or even to this Marcus Brody. But I can't.'

'Why not?' Indy asked.

'They would ask questions that I cannot answer,' he said simply.

'Questions about what?' Indy asked.

'Questions that private tourists do not worry about, but that officials have to ask. Questions about how I got it ... and whom I got it from,' said Sallah.

'Where did you get the ring?' When Indy saw Sallah hesitate, he added, 'Look, you can trust me. Honest. I don't want to get you in trouble. I just want to help you get out of this with clean hands ... and to make sure the ring gets into the right hands.'

Sallah still hesitated. Then the boys' eyes met. Sallah made up his mind.

'Yes, Indy, I do trust you,' he said. 'But there is nothing you can do. The ring came from my second cousin Abdul. He gave it to me to sell, knowing I can speak foreign languages and can deal with tourists. I agreed only because he is a relative.'

Indy raised his eyebrows, and Sallah admitted, 'Maybe I do get a commission, but it's a very small one.'

But Indy wasn't really listening. A new idea had struck him – a very exciting idea.

'Where did Abdul find the ring?' Indy spoke fast. 'Did he discover a tomb somewhere? That would be fantastic. There aren't many tombs left to be found.'

Sallah shook his head. 'My cousin does not go out in the desert. He is a hotel porter.'

'Then how . . .' Indy began.

Sallah spread out his hands palms upward in a gesture of sadness. 'You must understand, most Egyptians are poor. My cousin Abdul is very poor. A porter's wages are terrible. Abdul has a wife and a mother and a mother-in-law and nine children to support. I, too, have many mouths to feed,' said Sallah. 'My father died last year. I have four brothers and six sisters and my mother to support on very little money. So sometimes we do things we do not like to do.'

'What did Abdul do?' Indy's voice was not accusing. He suddenly felt like a filthy-rich spoiled American. Who was he to hand out blame?

'He went through the belongings of a hotel guest and found the ring,' Sallah said. 'He says that the guest must have robbed a grave to get it. It is no sin to steal from a thief.'

Indy nodded. 'I can see his point, though I can't say I approve. It would have been better if he had gone to the police.'

'How could he, even if he'd wanted to?' Sallah explained. 'He would have had to explain how he had found the ring. He would have lost his job.'

'But that doesn't stop us from blowing the whistle on the grave robber,' Indy said.

'Yes it does,' argued Sallah. 'As long as the ring is involved, so is my cousin. I cannot let that happen.'

Indy bit his lip. Then he smiled as the solution came to him. 'But suppose we find a different way to nail this grave robber. Suppose we get the ring back to him. Then we shadow him until we get something else on him. Don't you see, Sallah?' asked Indy. 'Then your cousin would be out of it. The ring would go to a museum. The tomb the guy robbed would be put on the map. And that thief would be sent where he belongs . . . jail.'

Sallah's face brightened. Then it fell. 'There is a problem. My cousin does not work in Cairo. He works in Luxor.'

'No problem,' said Indy. 'It just so happens I'm going to Luxor with Marcus Brody tomorrow. Can you get there on your own?'

'I have a great uncle who works on the railroad,' said Sallah. 'He can get me on the train without a ticket.'

'Then you're in this with me?' asked Indy.

'I'm with you,' said his new friend. 'Clearly we were brought together by fate for this noble purpose.'

'Well, maybe fate has brought us this far,' said Indy. 'But I've got a hunch that once we get to Luxor, we're on our own.'

Chapter
5

Luxor was over three hundred miles from Cairo. Sallah made the trip on the railroad that the British had built. Indy took the ancient route. He and Marcus sailed up the Nile.

The boat was a modern steamer that chugged steadily against the current, but around it in the sparkling dark blue water, Indy saw countless boats with single sails. Some were going with the wind up the river, others sailed downstream with the current. It was just as their ancestors had done from the beginning of history.

The river was low and the grass on the river banks was brown from the summer sun. Not until September would floodwaters pour down the Nile to turn the banks green again.

Every now and then there would be a break in one of the river banks, and Indy would spy barren desert beyond. He could see how much

Egypt depended on the Nile, how close it was to ruin without that precious water.

Indy asked Marcus if the Nile ever failed to flood at the end of summer.

'Sometimes, unfortunately,' Marcus answered. 'When there's a drought in the Ethiopian highlands, where the floodwaters originate. The result is disaster. Crops die and people starve. The ancient Egyptians did a lot of praying to their gods to keep that from happening.'

'I noticed all the temples we passed on the river,' Indy said.

'You'll see even more, bigger ones, in Luxor,' Marcus assured him. 'Luxor used to be called Thebes. It was the religious centre of ancient Egypt. The high priests of Thebes had as much power as the Pharaohs. Maybe more.'

'Sounds like an interesting place,' Indy said, looking upriver. They were due to arrive within the hour.

After a day and night on this boat, Indy was eager to stretch his legs. He was even more eager to join up with Sallah. He patted his pocket to make sure the ring was still there. It was.

'You'll be able to do a lot of sightseeing,' Marcus said. 'Unfortunately I won't be able to go with you. I have to meet with a wealthy Egyptian collector. He wants to become even more wealthy by selling his family collection to my musuem. I'll have to inspect the pieces. Then I'll have to haggle over the price. How these Egyptians love to haggle.'

'So I've heard,' said Indy.

'Unfortunately, he has the upper hand,' Marcus went on. 'Good pieces are in short supply, even in Luxor.'

'Luxor used to be a good spot to find them?' Indy asked with interest.

'A long time ago. There are many tombs across the river in hills to the west,' Marcus said. 'Pharaohs were buried in one valley. Queens in another. There was a valley for nobles, too. The tombs were piled high with treasures. Over the years they have all been cleaned out by looters.'

'All of them?' said Indy. 'Maybe some were overlooked?'

Marcus shook his head. 'Not a chance. Archaeologists have been over the area with a fine tooth comb. Still, the tombs sites are worth seeing. I'm sure you can find a tourist group going out to them.'

'Maybe I can hire a guide of my own,' said Indy. 'Things seem real cheap in Egypt.'

'I have to warn you,' said Marcus. 'The guides in Luxor have a bad reputation. Even the Egyptians call them thieves.'

Indy didn't mention that he already had a

guide waiting for him in Luxor. All he said was, 'Don't worry, I'll be careful.'

Much later that day, in Luxor as the sun set over the hills to the west, Indy repeated the same words to Sallah.

'Don't worry, I'll be careful.'

He had met Sallah in front of the hotel where Sallah's cousin worked. It was an impressive look-ing building, almost a palace. It stood surrounded by gardens on a small island connected to the town by a footbridge.

'We have a problem, Indy,' said Sallah, looking helplessly at the imposing building.

'What's that?' asked Indy.

'This place is for foreign tourists and maybe a few rich Egyptians,' Sallah explained. 'They would never let a kid like me in. And even if I sneaked in, the first employee who saw me would kick me out. Or worse.'

'But they'd let *me* in,' Indy said.

'I don't think it's a good idea for you to try to do this alone,' said Sallah. 'When you sneak into somebody's room, you should have another person to stand lookout outside. Just in case.'

Indy grinned. 'You sound like an expert.'

Sallah cleared his throat. 'I'm just saying what I've heard. You know, in the bazaar, you pick up all kinds of information.'

'Sure,' said Indy, still grinning. Then he said, 'Don't worry, I'll be careful. But tell me, in the bazaar, did you pick up any good tips about how to get into a hotel room?'

'No,' said Sallah. 'But I did pick up this from my cousin.' He handed Indy a key. 'It's a hotel pass key. It will open any door.'

'Great,' said Indy. 'I hope your cousin also gave you the room number.'

'Forty-nine,' Sallah said. 'And my cousin says the guy spends very little time in his room.'

'Then this will be a cinch,' said Indy. 'I'll go to the room. Knock on the door to make sure nobody's there. If he is, I'll pretend to have knocked on the wrong door. If he isn't, I go in. Then I stick the ring in the sort of place the guy might think he had put it by accident.'

'You sound pretty expert yourself,' Sallah commented. 'What bazaar do you go to?'

'Just call it native talent,' said Indy. 'Besides, this part is easy. The hard part comes when we have to tail this guy. By the way, what's his name?'

'That's a problem,' said Sallah. 'My cousin just knows the room number.'

'No big problem,' said Indy. 'I'll find out inside. See you in a little while.'

'Well, Indy, good luck,' said Sallah.

'Never wish a guy that,' said Indy. 'It makes it sound like I'll need it.'

Sallah waited outside underneath a tall tree ablaze with red flowers. Indy walked past the blue-uniformed doorman into the hotel lobby. He didn't hesitate. He went straight to the reception desk.

The reception clerk wore a pearl grey morning coat, striped trousers, a gleaming white shirt, and a flowing black tie. Indy was wearing slightly grimy khaki shorts and a tattered short-sleeved white shirt.

The clerk slowly looked Indy up and down. 'What can I do for you, *sir*?' he asked coldly.

'I'm supposed to deliver a message to —' Indy paused, and acted confused. 'Darn it I've forgotten the name. I just remember the room number — forty-nine. Could you help me, please? Do you know who that is?'

Suddenly Indy felt a hand on his shoulder.

'*I* can help you,' said a voice with a strong German accent. '*I* am living in Room 49.'

The large hand turned Indy around. Indy stared up at a powerfully built man in a white suit and white pith helmet. A monocle gleamed in one eye and the man wore a moustache waxed upwards into sharp points.

'Allow me to introduce myself,' he said. He

clicked his heels and made a short bow. 'Herr Doctor Professor Gustav von Trappen, at your service.'

The German's monocle glinted as he looked hard at Indy. 'And now you must help me. *Who are you? And what do you want with me?*'

Chapter
6

Trapped by von Trappen!

That was the first thing that popped into Indy's mind.

Then the name rang a bell.

He had seen that name back home, just after finding out about his trip. It was in a scholarly journal that his dad had left lying about in the living room. Indy picked up the magazine and skimmed through it. He stopped to read an article by Professor Gustav von Trappen. It was about Egyptian artifacts. Indy only managed to get half way through the article. It was very, very dull.

'Professor von Trappen!' he said. 'Boy, would my dad get mad at me for forgetting your name. He wrote it down for me so I would be sure to look you up when I got to Luxor. I'm afraid I left it behind at my hotel. Thank goodness I re-membered the room number. The hotel gave it to me when I telephoned to see if you were here.

I am *so* bad at names, dates, stuff like that. My dad says I'll never make it studying history.'

'And who is your father?' von Trappen asked.

'Henry Jones,' said Indy. 'Professor Henry Jones.'

'Ah, Professor Jones, the American,' von Trappen said. 'A good man in his field.'

'He says the same about you,' lied Indy. 'In fact, he says you are the very best.'

'Well, perhaps that is an exaggeration.'

But Indy could see the professor wasn't about to argue. That was the great thing about flattery. You couldn't pile it on too thick. Also it smothered any suspicions that you might be lying about something else.

Seeing the pleased smile on von Trappen's face, Indy decided to push his luck. 'My dad says you are doing sensational work in Egypt. He told me I should ask you about it.'

'Ah, word has reached America, has it?' the German's voice was smug. 'I suppose that is only natural. When one is as famous as I am, one's every move is reported.'

'Sure, you're big news in America,' Indy said, keeping a straight face. 'But tell me, have you made any big discoveries?'

Von Trappen gave a big sigh. 'Unfortunately, no. I thought I might find an untouched tomb in the Valley of the Kings. However, I was wrong. After months of work, I must admit failure.' Von Trappen shrugged. 'That is one of the risks of archaeology, but one must never be afraid to take chances. No risk, no reward.'

'So you didn't find anything?' Indy asked. 'No pottery? Or gold? Or jewellery?'

'Nothing of interest,' the professor sighed. 'Just a few broken pots and other minor relics.' Then he pulled out a pocket watch. 'Sorry, but I must be off. I have many affairs to wind up here, as I leave for Germany very soon. It was nice meeting you, Mr Jones. You may tell you father he should be proud to have such a perceptive son.'

'Gee, thanks a lot,' said Indy. As the German strode away, Indy added under his breath, 'Thanks for nothing.'

But the Professor had given him something . . . information he could use.

Indy shared it with Sallah when they met outside.

'This von Trappen said he's been digging in the Valley of the Kings,' Indy reported. 'That's where he must have found the ring. Probably a lot more, too. We have to get out there and check out his dig. I want to get the goods on that guy.'

'So you didn't like him much.' Sallah had seen the anger in Indy's eyes.

That fury blazed even brighter as Indy explained more. 'He's not just an ordinary grave robber. He's an archaeologist. That man is a traitor to his profession. And he's stealing not out of need, but greed.'

'Did you get the ring back to him?' asked Sallah.

'I didn't have a chance to,' said Indy. 'But don't worry. I won't use it as evidence and get your cousin involved. I'm sure we'll find something else. We'll have to move fast, though. Von Trappen was talking about packing up and going home.'

Sallah looked up at the darkening sky. 'It's too late to head out there now. We can go first thing tomorrow morning.'

'How do we get out there?' asked Indy.

'Leave that to me,' said Sallah. 'See you outside your hotel at eight.'

Indy pulled out a few dollar bills. 'In case you need them,' he said.

'I still have the money you gave me at the pyramids,' his friend reminded him. 'That'll be enough. More than enough. In fact, I'll bring you change.'

Sallah was as good as his word. The next morning, he handed Indy a bright shilling piece.

'Sorry if I'm a few minutes late,' he apologized.

'The bargaining took longer than I expected. These people in Luxor live up to their reputation. Very, very tricky. And you should have seen what the guy wanted to rent me. As if I was born yesterday.'

'Great work,' said Indy. 'I knew I could count on you. But I still have one important question.'

'What's that?' asked Sallah.

Indy looked at the long-legged, knock-kneed camel. It was snorting, its large teeth very much in evidence.

'How do I get up on that thing?'

Chapter 7

Sallah gave the camel a hard whack on its flank with a stick he was carrying.

'Sorry, I know it looks cruel, but it's the only way,' he said. 'Camels have thick hides, and even thicker skulls.'

The camel snorted, and the boy gave it an even harder whack.

Finally the camel got the idea. It lowered itself to its knees. Indy was able to climb into the saddle, and there was enough room for Sallah to climb on behind him. Another whack, and the camel rose to its feet.

'How far do we have to go?' asked Indy.

'About seven miles, after we take a ferry across the river,' Sallah said. 'The faster we go the better. The sun gets hotter and hotter as the day goes on.'

By the time they reached the Valley of the Kings, the sun was burning down. Indy was grateful that Sallah had thought to bring along two canteens of water. He wished Sallah had also provided a cushion for the saddle. He felt like he wouldn't want to sit down again for a week. A camel might be the best way to travel through this stretch of barren sand and rock, but it definitely wasn't the smoothest.

The dirt road they followed led into hills that looked like they belonged on the face of the moon. There was no trace of any green or growing thing. They saw only one sign of life. It was a solitary, scurrying, ghostlike grey fox.

'Boy, this place is *grim*,' Indy shivered. 'It sure is a perfect place for tombs.'

'The pharaohs thought so,' Sallah said. 'But for a different reason. These hills were to the west of Thebes. The sun set over them. The ancients looked on the sun as the symbol of life. To them the west was where the night of death began.'

'Hey, you're quite a guide,' said Indy.

'It's a good living,' Sallah grinned. 'Don't worry. No charge. I'm just practising.'

'When do we reach the Valley of the Kings?' asked Indy.

'We're entering it now,' Sallah told him. 'Maybe we should leave the camel here and go on foot the rest of the way. It will be easier to keep out of sight.'

'Great idea,' said Indy. He reached down to rub himself where it hurt the most.

They left the camel tethered in the shade of a rocky hillside. A wide gap in the hills opened before them. The Valley of the Kings.

As they moved down the valley they passed piles of rubble and deserted wooden huts.

'Napoleon brought the first archaeologists here with him,' Sallah said. 'Archaelogists have been digging here ever since.'

'They sure didn't clean up after they finished their work,' Indy remarked. 'Anyway, they're all gone now. All but von Trappen. It should be easy to spot his dig.'

'I already have,' said Sallah. 'Look!'

They were approaching a high barbed wire fence. As they came closer, they could see the large sign on it.

'*Eingang Verboten, Defense d'Entree, No Trespassing,*' read Indy.

'It says the same thing in Arabic,' said Sallah, scanning the writing on it.

'The way I see it, you shouldn't believe everything you read,' said Indy.

'Right,' agreed Sallah. He opened his leather pouch and took out a pair of wire cutters.

There was actually no one to see them. The boys crept around the large piles of rubble that littered the site. They saw only a couple of workmen lazily digging trenches.

'Looks like von Trappen was telling the truth,' Indy said. 'I guess he really is ready to shut up shop and go home. Maybe he just found that ring by chance. Nothing else seems to be here.'

'We should check out the whole site, though,' said Sallah. 'He's fenced off a big area.'

'We can do it faster if we split up,' said Indy. 'You go right. I'll go left. We'll meet back here in fifteen minutes.'

Sallah nodded and set off, carefully keeping out of sight. Indy did the same. Working his way around the piles of rubble, he found only more abandoned trenches and more rubble — the remnants of a dig that had gone nowhere and yielded nothing.

Then, as he cautiously skirted a big mound of rubble he saw something very different.

In neat rows before him were at least twenty tents. Like a small village, he thought to himself. A secret village. He wondered if anyone was at home.

Indy moved quickly and quietly to the nearest tent. Cautiously he parted an entrance flap and peeked inside.

In the semi-darkness the boy saw sleeping figures swathed in mosquito netting. He sniffed the musky scent of unwashed bodies. He heard snores and sleepy grunts.

He checked the next tent. More men were sleeping there.

It was then that he noticed the shovels and pickaxes stacked in front of the tents. There had to be a small army of workers here. Workers who slept in the day.

Workers who had to work at night.

Indy was about to hurry back and tell Sallah the news. Then a thought stopped him.

Sallah had a widowed mother to support. Brothers and sisters to help feed. If he got into trouble, a lot of people would suffer.

There was no sense in getting Sallah involved in what Indy could so easily do by himself. It must be up to him to find out what funny business was going on.

It turned out to be even easier than Indy had imagined. First Indy found out from Sallah as they rode back to Luxor where the camel had been rented. After he had said goodbye to Sallah for the day, he went to the camel dealer. The man agreed to rent the camel for the night for two shillings, after only fifteen minutes of haggling. Then it was a snap to sneak out of the hotel after saying goodnight to Marcus and pretending to go to bed.

It was easy, too, to find his way back to the Valley of the Kings. A full moon in a cloudless night sky lit the way.

And it was certainly very easy to see that something big was going on at von Trappen's dig.

The place was a hive of activity in the bright moonlight. Crouched behind a pile of rubble, Indy watched a steady stream of workers climbing down into a trench and coming out bearing loads of dirt and rock. They added the new loads to the rubble heaps all around the site. Indy saw the men carrying shielded kerosene lanterns down into the trench.

Then Indy's eyes widened.

Out of the trench came a man he could not mistake. Still in a white suit and pith helmet, a monocle in his eye. Von Trappen.

Von Trappen barked orders in German to a foreman who bowed before him. Then he went to a car where a uniformed chauffeur opened the rear door for him. A moment later, the car drove off, not using its headlights.

Indy watched the car vanish. Then he turned his attention back to the trench.

What was down there?

It had to be something far below the surface, with that amount of material being brought up.

And something very important, judging from the tone of von Trappen's voice.

If only Indy could get closer, so that he could peer over the edge.

Suddenly he saw how he could do it.

Fresh rubble was piled near the trench. He only had to cross a small stretch of open ground to reach its shelter.

Indy's muscles tensed. He waited ... and waited. Finally, when none of the workers was looking his way he ran for it.

He was sure he had made it.

Then his foot hit something.

The moment he heard the awful clatter, he knew what he had knocked over. Shovels and pickaxes had been stacked in the shadow of the rubble, where they couldn't be seen ... until it was too late!

Voices started shouting. The words were in German. Indy didn't know what they were saying, but it didn't sound like 'welcome'.

Skidding in the dust, Indy sharply doubled back, heading for the hole cut in the barbed wire fence.

He wriggled through, and he ran for his life.

Behind him he heard men coming after him.

Don't worry, he told himself. He was faster than they were. He was ...

Just then an arm reached out from the shadows and grabbed him. . .

. . . caught!

Chapter
8

'Come on – this way!' said a familiar voice.

Indy stared at the figure beside him. It couldn't be . . . but it was.

'Sallah!' he gasped. 'What are you . . .?'

'No time now. Tell you later,' Sallah whispered urgently.

Indy couldn't argue, Sallah had pulled him into the shadows, but any moment now his pursuers might spot them. He saw the light of lanterns coming from the dig. Indy also spotted the beam of light from a new-fangled electric torch. Von Trappen had the best equipment going.

Sallah led Indy to the other side of the rubble. Almost invisible in its shadow was a large horse. Sallah mounted it, then Indy climbed on behind to share the saddle. As they emerged into the moonlight, Indy saw they were astride a magnificent dark stallion.

'Better than a camel, huh?' said Sallah, as they raced out of the Valley.

'But where did you get him?' Indy asked.

'I . . . er . . . borrowed him,' Sallah chose his words carefully.

'Borrowed?' said Indy.

Sallah shrugged. 'It would have cost a fortune to rent him. I told you, the people in Luxor are thieves. The dealer has already got a shilling for that camel today. Borrowing this ho makes up for that highway robbery.'

By now they were well out of the Valley. No one was coming after them. The road ahead to Luxor stretched empty in the moonlight. Sallah slowed the stallion to a walk.

'By the way, how did you get out here?' Sallah asked.

'I rented that camel again,' Indy said. 'Which reminds me, it's still tethered back in the Valley. We have to go get it.'

'How much did you pay?' Sallah asked.

'Two shillings,' Indy admitted.

'That's very good, for a foreigner,' Sallah said. 'But for that price, the dealer will come and pick up the camel tomorrow himself. I'll talk to him.'

'Look, first I have to thank you for getting me out of that jam,' Indy said. 'But then I have to ask you, what were you doing out there?'

'I saw a bunch of tents with men sleeping in them today,' Sallah said. 'I figured something must be going on at night.'

'But why didn't you tell me?' asked Indy. He already could guess, though. The corners of his mouth were twitching in a grin.

'I didn't want to get you involved in any danger,' said Sallah. 'After all, I am an Egyptian. These people could be doing my country great harm. Like you said, they could be stealing our past. But you are an American. There is no reason for you to be so concerned.'

There was a moment of silence. Then Sallah started laughing. 'You saw the tents, too, and you kept your mouth shut. You did not want to get me involved, right?'

'I guess I was pretty dumb,' Indy admitted. 'I really care a lot about history, but I forgot that you might care even more than me when it comes to the history of Egypt. I apologize.'

'I apologize, too,' said Sallah. He turned around in the saddle and extended his hand. 'From here on in, we're in this together.'

'Together, all the way,' Indy agreed, as they shook hands.

Together – that's how they found themselves the next day. They were back on yet another camel heading for the Valley of the Kings.

Sallah had arranged with the dealer to return the camel that night, along with the camel that Indy had left tethered near the dig the night before. He had also beaten the man's price down to two shillings for everything. It took insults, wild wavings of hands, and threats of going to the police. The dealer had finally shrugged and agreed. They all had mint tea before the boys set off.

When they reached the tethered camel, they found it none the worse for being left untended. They tethered the second camel beside it.

'Camels can go without food or water for days,' Sallah said.

'I wish I could do the same,' said Indy. 'I'm thirsty already. The sun is hot today.'

'The sun's hot everyday,' Sallah agreed. He passed Indy a canteen of water. 'And it'll get hotter.'

'Just so long as we stay cool,' said Indy. He gulped some down, and passed the canteen back.

Sallah took a swallow. 'My throat's dry, too.' He grinned at Indy. 'Couldn't be that either of us is nervous, of course.'

Indy grinned back. 'Absolutely impossible.'

The barbed wire that Sallah had cut the day before had been replaced. Sallah cut it again.

'Von Trappen's men are efficient,' whispered

Indy. They cautiously made their way towards the trench where all the activity had been the night before. 'He really has them on their toes.'

'Fortunately they're all on their backs in their tents sleeping now,' said Sallah.

'Do you think they work at night because it's cooler then?' asked Indy.

Sallah shook his head. 'Diggers work early in the morning and late in the afternoon, when there is daylight. At night they might miss valuable finds.'

'Yeah,' said Indy. 'I have a hunch von Trappen has already found what he's looking for. He just doesn't want anyone to see how big his operation really is. Not after spreading the word that he's shutting up shop.'

'I hope that the excitement last night didn't make him post guards on the trench today,' said Sallah. 'Otherwise, we'll be able to get into the trench easy. The few diggers he has for show will be off for a meal and then a nap until four if they want to act convincing.'

Indy and Sallah crouched behind a heap of rubble near the trench. They watched the three diggers on duty, who did just what Sallah said they would.

'Now's our chance,' Indy said.

Swiftly they dashed for the trench, and jumped down into it. Then the boys froze.

'Uh-oh,' Indy murmured under his breath.

Von Trappen had posted a guard.

In the trench sat a man with a rifle beside him. Fortunately, he was asleep.

He is probably catching up on the sleep he missed last night, thought Indy. Still, he was dangerous. With that rifle, he meant business.

Sallah didn't seem worried, though. He picked up the rifle, looked it over, put it down. Then he picked up something else. An electric torch. He turned it on and sent its beam down the sloping trench. The light suddenly revealed a square-cut hole in the ground.

Carefully stepping around the guard, Indy followed Sallah to its edge.

The beam of light went down the hole.

'A stone stairway,' breathed Indy.

The boys went down the steps, Sallah leading the way with the torch. At the bottom they found a sloping underground passageway. They followed it further downwards.

'I wonder if this is what I think it is,' whispered Indy, not daring to say more. As if saying the word 'tomb' would make it disappear.

'I think it is,' Sallah whispered back.

It was.

There was a stone doorway standing open. And through that doorway was a sight beyond their wildest dreams. Indy and Sallah entered a world of magic.

Everywhere the lightbeam played was a fresh treasure ... beautiful golden couches ... statues of fabulous, monstrous animals made of precious metals and jewels ... kings carved out of ebony ... wall paintings of people who seemed ready to spring into life.

But nothing was as breathtaking as the lifesize statue of pure gold that stood in the centre of the crowded room. It made everything around it seem pale.

The statue was of a very young man, barely past boyhood. His slender body was naked to the waist. Above his delicately handsome face was a headdress adorned with a cobra's head rearing up. One of his hands was grasping a shepherd's crook — the ancients' staff of power. The other hand was extended with a finger pointing at the entrance — and at the boys.

'It's like he's accusing us of something,' Indy's voice was hushed.

'Or trying to tell us something,' whispered Sallah.

Suddenly a slamming sound as loud as a pistol shot echoed through the room.

The boys wheeled around. The stone door was shut.

From behind it a voice shouted something in German.

Sallah translated the gloating words.

'Welcome to the tomb. *Your* tomb.'

Chapter
9

Sallah shoved the stone door with his shoulder. It didn't budge. He really didn't expect it to. It was just something to do to put off having to admit there was nothing to do.

'The guard must have gone to get his boss,' Sallah said glumly. 'All we can do is wait for that von Trappen guy to show up. We can try to dream up a story, but I don't think he'll buy it.'

'It's not so bad,' Indy tried to assure him. 'We'll come up with something. All we have to do is keep our nerve and —'

Suddenly Indy stopped. His face went pale, eyes filled with panic.

Sallah followed his gaze. A long green snake slithered into his lightbeam. It was hissing angrily, flicking its forked tongue in and out of its mouth.

Sallah shrugged. He grabbed a golden shovel lying nearby, and chopped the snake in half.

Then he turned back to Indy. The colour was slowly returning to the boy's face.

'Hey, Indy, what's the trouble?' Sallah asked, puzzled. 'It was just a snake.'

'Uhhh, I've got this *thing* about snakes,' mumbled Indy. It was an embarrassing subject for him, but still a fact that his knees turned to water and his stomach turned over at the sight of any and all reptiles.

Indy changed the subject fast. 'When von Trappan arrives, we'll have to play it by ear. Until then, let's not waste our time in here. I want to take a good look around. It's a once-in-a-lifetime chance.'

'Maybe a last-in-a-lifetime chance,' Sallah said grimly. 'But you're right. This stuff is great. As great as Egypt once was.'

'And this statue is the greatest,' said Indy, letting the lightbeam play over it. 'What workmanship! Fantastic detail. It looks like it could move, could speak.'

'That's a royal headdress he's wearing,' Sallah drew close to examine it. 'He must have been a pharaoh. But he looks so young.'

'Hey, look at *this*,' Indy said. He was shining the light on the statue's pointing finger. 'See these little scrapes on the gold? I wonder if . . .'

Indy reached into his pocket. He pulled out

the ring stolen from von Trappen's room. The ring that the German had himself stolen from somewhere else.

Indy put the ring on the tip of the statue's finger and began to slide it on.

He was right. The ring was a perfect fit.

'So this is where von Trappen . . .' he began.

That was as far as he got.

The glow of his electric torch suddenly faded.

It faded in the dazzling light that flooded the room.

'The statue!' gasped Sallah.

The statue was a blaze of blinding light. Neither boy could turn his eyes away from it. They could not even blink. The light held them, drawing them into its power. The room they stood in was far away. They were soaring through endless light . . . endless space . . . endless time.

Indy tried to speak, but he could not. Neither could Sallah. They could only listen. Listen to waves of thought like pure music. A marvellous music that became a voice speaking words they could understand when it worked its magic on their minds.

'I am the Ka of Tutankhamon, once ruler of all Egypt,' the voice said. 'If you can hear me, nod your heads.'

Indy and Sallah both nodded.

'So be it,' the voice said. 'You have the gift of youth. Your inner selves are still open to the wonders of the universe. You have not yet closed the doors of your perception to things beyond your understanding. That is what mortals do as they grow old and proud and foolish. Now listen closely, as I tell you what you must know ... and do.'

Voiceless, Indy and Sallah again nodded.

'My mortal twin, the Pharaoh Tutankhamon, did his human best to assure me an eternal home,' the voice said. 'He was sickly from his birth, and only a boy when he came to the throne. He knew he would die young. Preparations for death filled his thoughts and his rule. He had his architects devise a tomb far better hidden than any other royal resting place. Then he had his priests create a curse far more powerful than any other for those who dared disturb it.'

The voice had been gentle. But now it grew as hard as iron, as threatening as thunder.

'You must tell those who have intruded here to repair the damage and depart. I will be merciful to them if they do. I will even pardon the man who took the sacred ring that grants me entry to this statue.'

'But if they do not obey, tell them this,' said

the voice. 'Those who came to steal from this tomb, and those who they serve, will suffer a curse. It will show no mercy and spare no victim. Nod if you will do as I say.'

Indy and Sallah nodded.

The voice and the light began to fade. There were only a few more words. 'You who returned the ring take it and put it on your finger. The power of Osiris will be with you as you do my bidding. When you have done so, return it once again.'

Then there was dead silence. The light of the electric torch looked feeble in the darkness after the brilliant light of the Ka.

'Did you see . . .?' Indy asked Sallah, too dazed to put the question into words.

'I sure did,' Sallah shook his head in awe.

'I wonder where the Ka went to,' said Indy.

'Maybe back to the royal casket, to rest with the remains of Tutankhamon,' Sallah suggested. 'It would be in another room, past another door. Royal tombs have a lot of rooms, to make it hard for thieves. Just like royal mummies have three or four caskets around them, one inside the other.'

'Maybe we can do a little more exploring,' Indy's eyes brightened at the thought.

'I don't think we have the time,' Sallah whispered. 'Listen.'

The door to the tomb was creaking open.

Indy took the ring off the statue's finger, and slid it on his own. It fitted. Tutankhamon must have been about his size. Ancient Egyptians were generally small, and Tutankhamon had been young.

'Now to give von Trappen the message,' Indy said. 'I hope Osiris does his stuff. I have a hunch we'll need all the help we can get.'

Chapter
10

As the tomb door creaked open, Indy did something he hated himself for doing.

The boy grabbed a piece of ancient fabric that had been lying intact for thousands of years in the airtight tomb. He ripped off a strip and wound it around the ring on his finger. There it looked like a bandage for a cut or burn.

He hoped the Ka would forgive him for this destruction. He could barely forgive himself, even though it was for a good cause. He had to keep von Trappen from spotting the ring and asking questions.

It didn't matter whether the German had noticed the ring was missing from his room or not. He would identify it instantly. Von Trappen had an archaeologist's trained eye, and there weren't two rings like this one in the world.

'Hope it works under wraps,' he murmured to Sallah.

'Maybe it will,' Sallah whispered back. 'Osiris is supposed to be almighty.'

The tomb door was open now. A rifle barrel thrust into the entranceway.

'Handen hoch!' a guttural voice shouted.

'Hands up,' Sallah translated, though the tone of the voice made the meaning clear in any tongue.

Indy and Sallah obeyed as the man came through the door, his rifle at the ready.

He wore native clothes and his skin was dark, but the features of his face as well as the language he used told Indy a different story.

The guy was German. His clothes were a disguise. His skin had been stained. Were all the other workers on the site German, too? Indy bet they were.

The man motioned with his rifle for the boys to exit the tomb. Sallah went first, Indy next. The man prodded Indy with his rifle to hurry him along.

Von Trappen was waiting for them outside in the trench. He wore a slouch hat now, a bush jacket, and twill trousers with high boots, but a monocle still glinted arrogantly in his eye.

Von Trappen's face lit up when he saw Indy. He smiled. It was the smile of a very large cat playing with a very small mouse in a tiny space

... a space with no escape routes. Indy almost expected to see him lick his thin lips under his waxed moustache.

'Ah, young Mr Jones, the student of history,' he said. 'What are you doing here? Pursuing knowledge perhaps?'

'Here goes nothing,' Indy silently said to himself.

Out loud he said to von Trappen, 'That's right. This native guide here offered to take me to see the Valley of the Kings. He showed me the tombs, though they wouldn't let us go into most of them. The lighting was bad in the ones I did see. Then I spotted this dig over here. My guide here, Sallah, warned me it was private property. But I insisted on taking a look. I guess that was pretty dumb. But I didn't think anyone would mind.'

'Mind? Why would I mind?' von Trappen said, his sneering smile growing wider. 'It is good to see a young person with such curiosity. What a good archaeologist you would have made when you grew up. What a pity that you won't.'

'Hey, look, I can see why you would be a little mad,' said Indy. 'But I didn't mean any harm. And of course I won't say anything to anyone about the stuff in the tomb, not that I saw much, it being so dark. My dad has told me how important it is to keep a big find very secret until you can research it.

'Otherwise you have to worry about reporters writing inaccurate stories,' Indy prattled on. 'Tourists would get in the way, and of course looters. So I promise to keep completely mum about it, for as long as it takes you to finish your work, even if it's years and years.'

'Well, that takes a load off my mind,' said von Trappen. 'But what about your guide here? We must find a way to shut him up. In ancient times, we could cut out his tongue, but nowadays we must do something more drastic.'

'Oh don't worry about Sallah,' Indy assured him. 'A few dollars will keep his mouth shut. You know these Egyptians. Anything for money.'

'That's right,' Sallah chimed in. 'A few dollars. Or pounds. Or marks. I don't ask much. Just a little bit for my widowed mother and my hungry brothers and sisters.'

Von Trappen's shoulders shook, his stomach heaved. He had to take his monocle from his eye to wipe away tears of laughter.

Then his outburst of merriment ended as suddenly as it had begun.

His face was cold and his voice was icy. 'What kind of fool do you take me for? You actually thought that I would ignore the attempt to break into here last night? You didn't imagine I would be ready for the next attempt?' His mouth curled in contempt. 'It is you who are the fools. Believing the guard outside the tomb was really asleep.'

Indy felt like kicking himself. Of course. The guard had been playing possum. Waiting for intruders. Looking to see who they were, what they wanted, and how far they would go.

Sallah made his try, *'Bitte, mein Herr, wir sind nur Kinder. Wir sind nicht schuldiq.'*

'So you are just poor innocent children?' said von Trappen.

'Jowohl, mein Herr,' Sallah affirmed.

'I must say, you are very clever for a native,' said von Trappen. 'You know English and German. Tell me, how many other languages can you lie in?'

Indy decided to play his last card in this losing game.

'Sallah knows ancient Egyptian, too,' he said. 'He translated the inscriptions in the tomb for me. He says they contained the most terrible curse he ever saw. A curse on anyone who disturbed the tomb. A curse much stronger even than the ones other pharaohs put in their tombs. I have to warn you about that. Maybe it would be better for everyone concerned if you sealed up the tomb again. Maybe you should just forget about the whole thing.'

'Of *course* I will,' von Trappen said in a mocking

voice. 'What a close call I had. Thank you so much for saving me, but let me give you a little token of my gratitude.'

He raised one large hand and spun Indy's head around with a vicious slap.

Dazed, Indy shook his head. Stars of pain danced in his eyes. Through these stars he saw the look of pleasure on von Trappen's face.

Smiling in anticipation of more, von Trappen raised his hand again and dealt Sallah a vicious blow.

Suddenly there was a blur of motion.

Von Trappen screamed as a thin line of blood appeared on his cheek.

Sallah turned to see Indy wielding a long thin whip.

As Sallah watched, amazed, Indy sent the lash across the face of the digger guarding them.

The digger dropped his rifle and both his hands flew to his face.

Indy grabbed the rifle, and covered von Trappen. 'You should always listen to old Egyptian curses,' Sallah said. Then he said to Indy, 'Where did you get the whip?'

'In the tomb,' said Indy. 'I picked it up after I bandaged my finger. It might be a few thousand years old, but it still works fine. A whip can come in real handy sometimes.'

Sallah nodded. 'So I see. I'll have to remember that for the future.'

Still holding his wounded cheek, von Trappen snarled, 'Future? Future? You want to know your future? Then look up above your head.'

Indy grinned. 'Good try, von Trappen. But you can't trick me that way. My eyes and this gun are staying right on you and your hired hand.'

'Uhh, Indy, you'd better look,' said Sallah in a weak voice.

Indy did.

Above them, on the edge of the trench, stood at least a dozen men. Their eyes were looking down. Their rifles were fixed on Indy.

Chapter
11

The first thing von Trappen did was take care of himself. He had one of his men run for a first aid kit. Carefully he applied antiseptic to the cut on his face, then he covered it with gauze and sticking plaster.

'You cannot be too careful about infection here in Egypt,' he told the boys. He touched the bandage on his face, testing it. He winced. The cut was painful. He glared at Indy and Sallah.

'You must make sure to destroy all germs before they can hurt you,' said von Trappen. Then smiled, the bandage making his smile uglier than ever. 'But that is true not only of germs. You cannot afford to be merciful to any enemies. The first rule of life is kill or be killed.'

Indy tried to argue. 'Can't you understand, we're not your enemies? We were trying to help you. We weren't kidding about the curse that the pharaoh laid down. There's no telling what might happen to you, but it's bound to be bad.'

'You expect me, a man of science, to believe in such mumbo-jumbo?' von Trappen said with renewed rage. 'I will show you what I think of this curse of yours, and I will show you a curse far more powerful than any curse a pharaoh's priest ever dreamed up. I will show you the punishment for those who meddle with *me!*'

He ordered two of his men to keep Indy and Sallah covered with their rifles. Then he barked commands to his other diggers. The men went into the tomb. They returned grunting and groaning under the burden they carried.

The golden statue of Tutankhamon.

'Beautiful, isn't it?' said von Trappen. 'Quite the most splendid piece of Egyptian art I have ever seen.'

'I can understand why you want to take it,' Indy said. 'It's a fabulous prize for an archaeologist. But it should stay in Egypt, in the hands of the Egyptians.'

'I assure you, it will.' Von Trappen smiled as though at a private joke.

With armed guards behind them, the boys followed von Trappen out of the trench. A truck was waiting with its cargo section covered by arching canvas. Von Trappen's men loaded the golden statue aboard. The boys and their guards followed, and the canvas flaps were closed behind them. Von Trappen sat in front beside the driver.

'At least we'll find out where von Trappen is storing the loot,' Indy said to Sallah.

Indy had checked out the guards to see if they knew English. They didn't, so he and Sallah were able to talk freely, although that was the only thing they could do. One of the guards kept an electric torch on them in the dark as the truck bounced along the dirt road. The other held a gun. With the safety catch off and his finger on the trigger the boys didn't have to be told to keep still.

'Von Trappen must have a warehouse to store all that stuff,' Sallah said. 'I wonder how he plans to keep it secret?' Then he brightened. 'Maybe he doesn't plan to keep it secret. Maybe he plans to make a big announcement. You know, invite reporters to see the stuff he's found. It would make him the most famous archaeologist in the world.'

'Sure, that's it,' continued Sallah, hopefully. 'He's keeping us prisoner until then, so we won't spoil his surprise. All that mean talk of his was just to scare us. He's that kind of nasty guy.'

Indy grimly shook his head, 'Hate to be a wet blanket, Sallah, I've already thought of that and it doesn't make sense. No archaeologist removes things from a tomb without carefully taking photos and measurements of everything as he originally found it. His name would be mud in the profession. No, von Trappen is what we thought from the start – a common grave robber. He stands to make a mint if he sneaks the loot out of the country. I just wonder how he plans to do it.'

Indy got his answer when the truck braked to stop. The guards herded the two boys outside.

They had reached the Nile. A gleaming white ocean-going yacht was moored to the bank. Her spotless brass fittings blazed in the Egyptian sun.

'Superb, isn't she?' said von Trappen. 'A masterpiece of modern engineering, equipped with everything an archaeologist might need. She was a gift from the Imperial German Government, an example of our beloved Kaiser Wilhelm's support of science. It won him much praise.'

'And this is how you plan to repay him?' said Indy. 'I thought you Germans were supposed to respect your Kaiser.'

Von Trappen drew himself up to his full height. He stood at stiff attention as he spoke. 'Respect the Kaiser? Of course I do. I am his most loyal subject – as you will soon find out.'

Indy could see that von Trappen was telling the truth as soon as they boarded the yacht. The crew were not in disguise. They wore the white uniforms of the German navy, complete with webbed belts and pistols in gleaming leather holsters.

'We are safe from prying eyes here,' von Trappen said. 'I have all roads to this area guarded. I have bought the land around and moved off the farmers. In case you have any ideas about trying to escape, I thought I would just let you know there is no way out.'

They went below decks, and entered a large room dominated by a giant furnace.

'This furnace is an archaeologist's dream,' said von Trappen. 'I can forge any tools I might need in a dig, and test any metal objects I might find. It was reported on with great admiration in scientific journals.'

He patted the furnace fondly. 'Of course, there are uses that hadn't occurred to the writers of those journals ... uses that the Imperial government did not mention. Can you guess what they might be?'

'I'd rather not,' Indy said. He didn't like the glittering look he saw in von Trappen's eyes. It reminded him of a vulture eyeing its prey.

At that moment the statue of Tutankhamon was brought into the room by a group of sweating diggers. They set it down by the furnace door.

Von Trappen ran his hand over it tenderly.

'Solid gold. It will melt down beautifully. What a nice pile of ingots it will make.'

Indy choked with horror – and anger. 'Melt it down? That's the most terrible thing I've ever heard.'

'Is it really?' said von Trappen. He touched his bandaged cheek. Next he reached out and gave Indy's cheek a vicious pinch. Smiling at Indy's gasp of pain, he did the same to Sallah. 'Now I wonder what you would say if I told you the furnace's other use. How very efficiently it can dispose of a corpse . . . or even two.'

Chapter
12

Indy had read somewhere that the Kaiser was
fascinated by uniforms. The German Emperor
liked to put on a new one for every occasion.

Von Trappen had the same style moustache as
his ruler, and the same taste in clothes.

He walked out of the ship's workroom, leaving
the boys under guard. When he returned, he no
longer looked like an archaeologist on a field trip.

Von Trappen wore a naval officer's white uniform, complete with epaulettes and peaked cap. His
jacket displayed a collection of ribbons and
medals of every colour, size and shape. It looked
like a pawnshop window.

The sailors guarding Indy and Sallah saluted
Von Trappen smartly when he entered the room.
He responded with a casual flip of a white-gloved
hand to his forehead. He barked out orders in
German. The sailors clicked their heels and
obeyed.

'This can't be happening!' Indy said as the sailors slid the golden statue into the furnace. He turned to von Trappen. 'You can't do this!'

'Can't I?' von Trappen's voice was icy cold. 'Watch and see.'

'But *why*?' Indy demanded. 'Okay. I can understand you smuggling the statue out, maybe for yourself, maybe for greedy collectors. Even some museums would shell out a fortune for it, and not ask how you got it, but melting it down? The gold bars wouldn't be worth nearly as much as a priceless gold statue. Besides, how can you as an archaeologist bring yourself to do it? Why, it's . . . it's . . .'

Indy paused. He couldn't find a word to express his disgust.

'A monstrous crime?' suggested von Trappen. 'A sacrilege? An unpardonable sin against science? For an archaeologist, yes . . . but not for a captain in naval intelligence under orders of the Kaiser himself. I am just doing my duty.'

'You mean, you're a secret agent?' Sallah gasped, his eyes widening. 'And I always thought they wore trenchcoats and stuff like that.'

'Actually, I do have a trenchcoat,' von Trappen laughed. 'I have used it in London several times, but mostly the climate where I work is too warm for it. The Middle East is my speciality as an archaeologist, and the place where I can do the most for my King and country.'

'But what are you doing here?' asked Indy.

'I should think you could guess, a smart boy like you,' von Trappen said.

'I can,' Sallah said.

Von Trappen lifted his eyebrows. '*You*? Really?'

'It has to have something to do with the Suez Canal,' said Sallah. 'The English have so many troops here to protect it. That must mean somebody would want to get at it.'

'You're very clever for a native,' said von Trappen. 'Yes, somebody might want to get at it.'

'Sure,' Indy said. He remembered what Marcus Brody had told him back in Cairo. 'England would be cut off from most of its empire without the Canal. That would make a big difference if there's ever war in Europe.'

'Not *if* there's war, but *when* there's war,' von Trappen said. His eyes gleamed fanatically. 'It is Germany's destiny to rule Europe, and England leads the nations stubbornly trying to stop us. They must be swept away. There will be war, and it will be short and sweet.'

Indy started to think of questions he could ask to make von Trappen spill more about what he was up to in Egypt. However, no questions were needed. Von Trappen was as eager to talk about his mission as he was to show off his uniform and medals.

'When victory is ours, I will wear the Iron Cross,' he said, his voice swelling with pride. 'The world will learn I was no mere archaeologist scratching in the dirt of the past. I was the man who won the war, the man who stored the explosives that blew up the Canal and crippled England. The man who, on his own, provided the weapons and the gold to finance the native uprising that made it even easier.'

'So you're going to store guns and explosives in the tomb, and then cover it up again,' Indy slowly nodded. It was becoming clear. 'That's why you said you hadn't found anything.' Then his face clouded with puzzlement. 'But one thing I don't understand. How could you be so sure you would find the tomb?'

Von Trappen chuckled. 'I am glad you asked. You see, I was sure I *wouldn't* find a tomb. It is such a wonderful joke.'

'Huh?' said Indy. 'I don't get it.'

'The American archaeologist Davis, after digging for years, announced that all tombs had been found,' said von Trappen. 'Davis had the government concession to dig in the Valley, and

78

he warned me I was wasting money when I paid him to let me dig there. I planned merely to dig holes to store the munitions. Finding the tomb was an accident. Some might call it luck, but it is proof to me that the gods are on Germany's side ... especially the god of war. The tomb will be the perfect hiding place for our secret armoury in Egypt.'

'And the relics – you're going to *destroy* them,' said Indy.

Von Trappen shrugged. 'I have no choice. I will use the gold and jewels to stir up opposition to England in Egypt. Perhaps I can even fuel a native rebellion. I will dump what's left into the Nile. There must be nothing to lead to the armoury, no trace left of the discovery.'

Von Trappen paused, then added, 'I must admit, though, I could not resist taking a trinket as a souvenir, a rather charming ring. Perhaps I will give it to a museum after the war, or I might even wear it myself.'

'You really expect to get away with this?' said Indy.

'Somebody is bound to talk,' Sallah declared. 'There are too many men involved. Look, let's make a deal. Let us go and we won't say a word about any of this. We'll even keep quiet about the statue. You can seal up the tomb again. Sail away and tell the Kaiser the scheme didn't pan out. Then you're home free.'

'You natives, always haggling – even though you have nothing to bargain with,' said von Trappen with contempt. 'I have no worry about my men talking. They are good Germans, not worthless natives. As for you two blabbing, I don't . . .'

At that moment, he was interrupted by one of the sailors who saluted, then reported something in German.

Von Trappen said to the boys, 'Now you will see what German determination and genius can do. My engineer worked day and night to convert the furnace into an efficient smelter. Come, let us look at the results.'

The boys were marched to the furnace. There one of the sailors reached for a spigot on the side, but von Trappen waved him away. Von Trappen wanted to be the one who committed the terrible crime.

His face lit up as a stream of molten gold poured into a mould. When it was filled, the spigot was turned off, and the mould set aside to cool. Beaming, von Trappen stepped back and let the sailor take over the job.

'So beautiful, the most beautiful thing on earth.' Von Trappen gazed at the mould he had filled.

Indy stared at the molten metal. Then he thought of the masterpiece, the marvel that no one would see again. 'Horrible, the most horrible thing I've ever seen,' he said.

'Horrible?' said von Trappen. 'I am so sorry to have offended you. I can only promise that you and your native friend will not have to see something that you would find even more horrible . . . ashes. Human ashes that will join all the others that have vanished into the Nile.'

Von Trappen turned and gave a command to a sailor. The sailor approached, took a Luger pistol from its holster, and handed it to von Trappen.

'Another triumph of German engineering,' von Trappen said, looking at the Luger in his hand as fondly as he had gazed at the gold. He moved it up and down, testing its weight and balance. He snapped off the safety catch and his finger curled around the trigger. Then he looked at Indy and Sallah.

'Now tell me, boys,' he demanded. 'Which one of you wants to go first?'

Chapter
13

Before Indy could make a move, Sallah stepped forward.

'I'll go first,' he said.

Von Trappen looked surprised.

'I must say, you're very brave for a native,' he said.

He levelled his Luger to point at Sallah's heart.

'And how's this . . . for a native?' Sallah said, as he grabbed the mould full of molten gold by its handle.

In one smooth motion Sallah sent the molten gold flying out in an arc that caught von Trappen and the sailors beside him in their faces.

'Aaaghh!' their screams mingled in the air. Von Trappen's Luger clattered to the floor. Sallah and Indy dashed for the door.

When they reached the ship's narrow passageway, Indy slammed the door behind them. If only the door had a bolt on the outside, he

82

thought, they could lock von Trappen and his men inside. But no luck. No bolt.

Then Indy saw a long-handled axe hanging on the passageway wall. It had been put there in case of a fire emergency.

His eyes flicked back to the door, which opened outward from the room. Maybe, just maybe . . .

Sallah, who was ahead of him, grabbed the axe. He put one end against the door, and wedged the other against the facing passageway wall.

'Great minds think alike,' said Indy.

'Right now, my only thought is getting off this ship,' his friend replied.

'At least we've bought some time,' said Indy. 'It'll take them a while to bash the door off its hinges.'

From inside the room came the sound of von Trappen and his men trying to do just that.

'Come on, let's head for the deck,' said Indy. 'It should be dark by now. Maybe we can sneak off the ship.'

They went up the metal ladder to the deck, two rungs at a time. Indy poked his head up through the hatchway. It was night, but again moonlight was flooding down.

'At least the coast is clear,' whispered Indy. He went out on to the deserted deck, crouching low.

Sallah followed, doing the same. Keeping in shadows as much as they could, they made it to the gangway.

'Rats, it's guarded,' said Indy, peering down it.

Two sailors with rifles in their hands stood on the shore in front of the gangway.

'They'll see us if we go over the railing on the shore side,' Indy whispered. He thought for a second. 'Say, Sallah, can you swim?'

'I can,' Sallah said. 'But . . .'

'Great.' Indy had decided. 'We can go over the other side of the ship.'

'The trouble is . . .' Sallah began again.

Again he had no chance to finish his sentence.

The sound of von Trappen's voice, shouting in German, filled the air.

The guards started running up the gangway to help their commander.

Meanwhile, von Trappen and the two sailors with him had come up through the hatchway. They spotted the two boys.

'They've cut us off from the river,' Indy said. 'Come on, we'll try that other hatchway over there.'

He and Sallah made it through the hatchway and down a ladder leading further below decks.

They were in a large hold lit by a dim electric light. Wooden crates were stacked to the ceiling.

'Wonder if this is what I think it is?' said Indy, eyeing them.

'Bet it is,' said Sallah.

With feverish haste the boys pried open one of the crates.

'Dynamite,' said Indy.

'Enough to blow up the Suez Canal,' Sallah was looking with awe at the crates piled high around them.

At that moment von Trappen's voice came down through the hatchway.

'Come on out,' he demanded, 'or we will come down and get you. There is no way out of that hold. To make your surrender simpler, I will make you an offer you cannot refuse. Give us no more trouble, and your deaths will be quick and painless, but try any more tricks, and it will not be your corpses we put into the furnace. *We will burn you alive!*'

Sallah was startled when Indy called back, 'Okay, okay, we're giving up! You win!'

Then Sallah saw Indy give him a big wink.

Reaching into the crate, Indy pulled out a stick of dynamite. He stuck it in his belt and went hand over hand up the ladder.

Sallah started to say something, but it was too late. Sighing, he followed Indy up. He didn't want Indy to have to face alone what was coming.

When they stood on deck, von Trappen smiled triumphantly. 'I'm happy you have seen reason,' he sneered.

'Are you happy to see *this*,' Indy spat out, as he whipped the dynamite stick from his belt. 'All of you drop your guns or I blow us all sky high. Believe me, I'll do it. I've got nothing to lose.'

The guns fell to the deck, and Indy's face broke out in a grin.

That grin lasted about five seconds.

That was how long it took for von Trappen to see clearly the dynamite stick in Indy's hand.

'Go ahead, explode it,' said von Trappen, laughing. 'You have no firing cap.'

'Oops,' said Indy, and raced for the railing above the river.

'Didn't have a chance to tell you,' said Sallah, close beside him.

'At least we can get into the river,' said Indy, as a gunshot whistled past his ear.

He was over the railing in an instant, swimming as hard as he could.

Sallah kept up the pace beside him.

A searchlight from the yacht was sweeping over the water to search them out.

A machine gun was firing, spraying bullets into the water, closer and closer.

'I think we're going to make it,' Indy gasped.

'We're almost out of range. We're . . .'

He stopped. In the moonlight he saw eyes staring at them . . . lots of eyes. Eyes in evil-looking heads with long snouts and hideously smiling jaws, which cut swiftly through the water. All heading straight for the two boys.

'Are they . . .?' Indy choked out.

'That's right,' said Sallah. 'That's the other thing I didn't get to tell you. *Crocodiles!*'

Chapter
14

Indy stared with horror at the crocodiles moving through the water towards them. Their eyes were yellow, their hideous skins greyish-green in the moonlight.

He turned in the water to start swimming away. Then he saw the searchlight moving towards them. It was followed by splashing bullets as the machine gun blasted away.

There was nowhere to go.

The searchlight reached them as the machine gun paused in its chatter to receive a fresh belt of bullets. Indy heard von Trappen's laughter in the night.

Indy gritted his teeth. Von Trappen saw the spot they were in, he was enjoying his moment of triumph, the moment just before either his bullets or the crocodiles made the kill.

There was nothing Indy could do. Just see red. Time to make one final gesture of defiance.

Treading water, he raised his fist and shook it at von Trappen.

'What the . . .?' he managed to say, before his voice was drowned out in a deafening explosion.

Von Trappen's yacht erupted into a huge fireball. Indy averted his head from the blinding sight. The crocodiles were turning tail in terror and speeding away.

'Did you see what I did, just before the big bang?' Indy asked Sallah, who was treading water beside him.

'I saw it,' Sallah said. 'No one would ever believe it . . . but I saw it.'

Both of them looked at the fist that Indy had held up in defiance. They stared at the ring on Indy's hand. The wrapping had come loose in the water. They remembered seeing a quick flash of light. It had shot out from that ring like a lightning bolt to score a direct hit on von Trappen and his yacht.

'The curse of the pharaoh,' Indy breathed.

'The power of Osiris,' Sallah said in the same awed voice. 'It's still there.'

Then Indy recovered from his shock. 'But we're still *here*,' he said. 'Let's get to shore quick, before those crocodiles come back.'

They hauled themselves, dripping, up on to the river bank. They looked for traces of the yacht. They found only scraps of charred wood thrown up on the shore. Any other wreckage was already moving downstream on the river current. The Nile, as it had done for thousands of years, was sweeping itself clean.

When they made their way down the road towards Luxor, they realized that it had been an even cleaner sweep than they thought. They found von Trappen's truck empty, his guard posts deserted. He must have had his whole command on the yacht.

'That's that for von Trappen and his crew,' said Indy, trying to sound cool. No sense in letting Sallah see how much he was shaking inside. Besides, there was still work to do. 'Now we just have to worry about the diggers on the site. We'll head back there first thing tomorrow. I have to get back to the hotel now — or else Marcus will have kittens worrying about me.'

Sallah thought for a moment. Then he said, 'You can sleep late tomorrow. I'll handle it.'

'How?' asked Indy.

'You'll see,' said Sallah. 'I'll pick you up tomorrow about noon. Right now, I'll drive you back to your hotel.'

'You know how to drive? I've got to hand it to you, Sallah. You're pretty resourceful,' Indy said. 'For a native, of course,' he added with a big grin.

Indy saw just how resourceful Sallah really was the next day when they drove to the dig.

Not a digger was left there.

'I have an uncle who's a policeman,' Sallah explained. 'In Egypt, relatives do each other little favours. I had him do me the little favour of coming out here this morning and telling the diggers that von Trappen and his yacht had blown up. He then demanded to see their identity papers. When they showed him forged ones, he told them they would all soon be in Egyptian jails. They may have been German, but they knew about Egyptian jails. They actually offered my uncle a bribe to let them clear out. Of course, only as a favour to me did he accept it.'

'I hope they don't spread the news about the tomb,' said Indy.

'I don't think they'll want to have anything more to do with Egypt,' said Sallah. 'My uncle said they looked real happy to be able to clear out. Anyway, I have a hunch von Trappen didn't tell them much about his discovery. He wasn't the kind of guy who liked to share things.'

'Time will tell,' said Indy. 'We can just wait and see, and do what we have to do. Get the ring back to its owner, then close up the tomb again.'

Sallah's face lit up. 'Then you're not going to

report the discovery. I was hoping you'd say that.'

'I want to be an archaeologist when I get older, but first I have to make sure I do get older,' Indy said. 'I saw what the Ka's curse could do. The sooner I give him back his ring, plus his peace and quiet, the safer I'll feel.'

'I'm with you,' Salah said, and headed with Indy for the tomb.

When they swung open the tomb door, they found it as they had left it, except for the empty space where the golden statue had been.

Indy had picked up an electric torch that had been abandoned inside the tomb near the door. He let the light beam play around the room as he looked for the proper place to deposit the ring.

Sallah went and tapped on the wall on the far end of the room. It made a hollow sound.

'The pharaoh's casket must be in a chamber behind it,' he said. 'That's the way these tombs are usually built.'

'That's where the Ka is,' Indy said. 'And where the ring should go.'

Indy picked up a golden shovel. Sallah picked up a golden spear. Working together they battered a hole through the thin masonry. They squeezed through it one after the other.

They were in a rectangular room with yellow

coloured walls. On the walls were vivid pictures of the pharaoh, his queen, his nobles, and his many gods. Statues of gods were placed in niches in the walls.

Sallah looked at those statues and said, 'It's a real tough crew that the priests put together here. They sure wanted to make the curse against intruders stick.'

Indy went to a huge stone block that dominated the room. 'The pharaoh's coffins and his mummy have to be inside this. His Ka, too.'

'Right,' Sallah agreed.

'I don't think we ought to disturb him any more,' Indy said. 'We'll just leave the ring on top of the stone and get out of here.'

Sallah glanced up at the menacing figures of the gods. 'Good idea,' he said.

Indy took the ring from his finger and laid it on the stone. Once again the dazzling light filled the room. Again a voice filled the minds of the two boys.

'You have performed your work well. Now please take this ring as your reward. It will no longer have the power of Osiris, but it will always remind you of what you have achieved and what you have learned.'

The light faded, leaving only the dull glow of the electric torch.

'Guess we can't say no,' said Indy, picking up the ring. He held it out to Sallah. 'You take it. You did as much as I did, and this is your country. I don't like the idea of foreigners taking relics out of their native lands.'

'I don't either,' said Sallah. 'But in this case, I make an exception. I want you to take it, as a souvenir of my country, and as a token of my friendship.'

'I can't,' Indy protested.

'You must,' Sallah said, in a voice which accepted no argument. 'In Egypt, there is no greater insult than refusing a gift.'

'What can I say ... except thanks,' said Indy. He slipped the ring back on his finger.

'And now let's get out of here, before our good luck runs out,' said Sallah.

'I'm ready,' said Indy. They slipped through the hole they had made repaired the damage as best they could, then left through the tomb door. They turned to swing the door shut. Then they turned again.

'Don't look now, but I think our luck has run out,' Indy whispered.

A digger was standing facing them in the trench. He was raising his rifle, and his eyes were burning with hate.

Chapter
15

Indy looked into the digger's menacing eyes and saw death staring out of them.

The rifle was pointed right at his heart.

'No use. It's all over,' he said to himself, waiting for the bullet.

Then Indy saw the digger's eyes roll upwards in their sockets. The rifle dropped to the ground. The digger's body collapsed on top of it.

The boys ran to him.

Indy touched his face. It was burning hot.

'The guy's got something,' he said.

'And I know what it is,' said Sallah. 'Get back!'

Sallah grabbed Indy by the shirt. He yanked him away from the digger, who lay helplessly shaking with chills and fever.

'See those sores behind the ears,' said Sallah. 'They're on other parts of his body too. They mean one thing. Plague.'

'Plague?' Indy gasped.

'Bubonic plague,' Sallah said grimly.

The name rang a bell in Indy's mind. A funeral bell. 'The Black Death,' he said, thinking of the hideous disease that had killed millions in the Middle Ages. 'I didn't think it was still around.'

'It is, especially in Egypt,' Sallah said. He saw how pale Indy's face was, and reassured him. 'Don't worry. You don't get it by just being near a victim. It's spread by ticks and fleas.'

'We'll have to do something for this guy,' said Indy, getting a hold on his nerves. 'He's in agony.'

'He won't be much longer,' said Sallah. 'He's too far gone. The only thing we can do is make sure his corpse is burned fast.'

Indy shook his head sadly. 'He must have sneaked back here to get some loot. He got something else instead.'

'He must have had it for a while,' said Sallah. 'My guess is that he's had it ever since he broke into the tomb. Ever since he upset the Ka.'

A shiver ran through Indy. 'The curse. That's it.' Indy shivered, '*Brrr*. I wouldn't want to be in the other diggers' shoes right now.'

'Me neither,' agreed Sallah. 'But that reminds me, we'd better get the tomb covered up again fast, before the Ka gets impatient.'

'The question is how?' Indy said. 'We can't do

it ourselves, and we don't have enough money to hire anyone.'

Sallah pursed his lips thoughtfully. 'Well,' he finally said, 'I have a few relatives who might help.'

Indy gave a smile of relief. 'I bet you do.'

Indy stood with Sallah at the end of the next day and watched the last of Sallah's relatives depart. Indy asked, 'Where did they all come from?'

Sallah shrugged. 'We Egyptians have big families and, as I said, we help each other.'

'I'll say,' Indy said.

A small army of men, women and children had arrived at the site on horseback, muleback, camel-back and foot. They left no trace of von Trappen's dig behind when they left. A small mountain of rubble lay over Tutankhamon's tomb.

'I know I shouldn't ask this about your relatives,' Indy said. 'But do you think they'll all keep quiet about the tomb?'

'I'm not insulted,' Sallah assured him. 'They're only human, and some of them are more human than others, but after I told them about the curse, they'll respect the Ka's wishes. Especially since I used what happened to von Trappen and the digger they saw here to back me up.'

Indy and Sallah rode back to Indy's hotel on

the camel they had rented. By now they were steady customers. The camel dealer gave them a cut rate.

The two boys were talking about what they might do the next day when Marcus Brody came running up to them.

'Indiana,' he said, out of breath. 'Where have you been? I've been looking everywhere for you.'

'I've been out to the Valley of the Kings, seeing the sights,' Indy told him. 'Sallah here has been my guide. He's the best. He was just describing the temple in Luxor we might go to tomorrow.'

'Ah, the temple of Karnak, a very great sight indeed,' said Marcus, nodding his head. But then he shook his head decisively. 'Unfortunately, you will have to miss it. We're leaving Luxor tonight.'

'You've finished your business already?' Indy said.

'Almost all of it,' Marcus said. 'There were only a couple of pieces worth thinking about. As I told you, the best are long since gone, but that's not the real reason for getting out of here fast.'

'Then what is?' Indy asked.

'A party of tourists, Germans, I think, have come down with the plague. Of course, they were quarantined instantly. There's not much chance of it spreading, but I don't want to take any chances at all. You are in my care. I don't want you to run the least risk of danger.'

'Right,' said Indy.

'So please go to your room and start packing immediately,' Marcus commanded.

'Will do,' said Indy. Of course he took time to say goodbye to Sallah before he left.

The two of them shook hands.

'Thanks for everything,' Indy told him.

'That goes double for me,' Sallah said. 'I'll be seeing you.'

'You know, I have a hunch you will,' said Indy.

He was telling the truth. As he watched Sallah ride off on the camel, Indy felt absolutely sure that he and Sallah would meet again. Somehow. Somewhere. Someday.

His thoughts were interrupted by Marcus.

'I see you didn't take my advice,' Marcus said.

'About what?' Indy asked.

'That ring on your finger.' Marcus sighed. 'I bet somebody palmed that off on you as a genuine ancient relic. I hope you didn't get robbed too badly.'

'Marcus, how can you say that?' said Indy, raising his eyebrows in protest. 'I just picked it up as a cheap souvenir. Even I could see it's a fake.'

As they walked into the hotel to pack, Marcus said sadly, 'Did you hear about the tragedy a couple of nights ago?'

'No I didn't.' Indy sensed what was coming.

'The great archaeologist, Gustav von Trappen, was killed when his yacht exploded. He must have been carrying dynamite for excavation work. Poor chap, what a terrible end to a glorious career. Especially since his last expedition was ending in failure. Everyone told him there were no more royal tombs to be found in Egypt, but he wouldn't listen. He only admitted defeat last week.'

'Gee, that's a tough break,' Indy agreed.

'Yes, the golden age of discovery is over,' sighed Marcus. He put his hand sympathetically on Indy's shoulder. 'I'm afraid that if you want to be an archaeologist, you can't expect excitement or adventure. There's none left in the modern world.'

Indy nodded.

'I guess you're right,' he said. Meanwhile, Indy kept his ring finger and the one next to it crossed.

HISTORICAL NOTES

In 1914, Germany and Great Britain did go to war. For four years World War I raged around the globe. In 1918, Germany was defeated and the German Kaiser lost his throne.

In 1922, a British expedition discovered Tutankhamon's tomb. Those in charge were puzzled by the fact that there were signs of the tomb being broken into before, but very little seemed to be missing. This fact was never satisfactorily explained. After the discovery, a number of people connected with the expedition met with unfortunate ends. Some said this was the result of an ancient curse but, of course, respectable scientific opinion has dismissed this idea as nonsense.

Young Indiana Jones and the Plantation Treasure by Rob McCay   014090218X

Young Indy Jones takes on more than he bargained for when he decides to help a beautiful young woman find a cache of treasure hidden by her late grandfather. The old man had been a plantation owner in South Carolina before the American Civil War. With the help of his journal, Indy and Lizzie set out to trace a former slave from the plantation, in whose hands lies the secret of the hidden treasure. But the intrepid boy is soon to discover that they are not the only ones on the trail . . .

Publishing date: May 1990

Young Indiana Jones and the Secret City by Les Martin   0140902163

Having witnessed the bizarre activities of an ancient sect posing as Whirling Dervishes, young Indy Jones finds himself in deadly danger during a trip to Turkey. Indy and his friend, Herman, are forced to fight for their lives in the vast maze of rooms and tunnels of a secret underground city. the rulars of this dark realm need only the blood of an innocent child to complete their evil rituals . . .

Publishing date: August 1990

Young Indiana Jones and the Circle of Death by Rob McCay

0140902171

A visit to an ancient British monument sparks off an unexpected adventure for Indy and his friend, Herman. A series of mysterious accidents have befallen a group excavating
the lonely site of Stonehenge. Rumours of black magic and supernatural incidents on Salisbury Plain lead Indy to investigate the history of the standing stones but as the darkest day of the year approaches, the Winter Solstice, the boys find their lives threatened by the Dark Druids, an evil sect with an unhealthy interest in human sacrifice!

Publishing Date: October 1990

Built to Last - 25 Years of the Grateful Dead by Jamie Jensen

0140902198

Not may rock groups have the insperation or the stamina to stick it out for 25 years, but then the Grateful Dead have never been just another rock 'n roll band. Ever since they burst onto the music scene in the psychedelic 1960s, the Grateful Dead have been doing things their own way and their unconventional approach to making music has earned them the unquestioning devotion of legions of fans around the world. Focusing on the unique experience of the Dead live in concert, with scores of photographs never seen before and interviews conducted on the eve of the first concert of the tour, this incredible book will put you in front-row centre at some of the best of the 2000-odd shows the Grateful Dead have played.

Bright Lights - A Ray Banana Adventure by Ted Benoit   0140901949

A complicated thriller comic of devious twists and turns, Bright Lights features Ray Banana, a cool American dude in shades, the sort of guy you won't forget. Screeching through the streets of Paris in his convertible, Ray finds himself caught up in drugs and murder intrigue as he hunts for a missing person, the famous painter Zelantius.

Electric Lullaby - A Ray Banana Adventure by Ted Benoit   0140901957

A chilling thriller comic of the not-too-distant future, Electric Lullaby features Ray Banana, a crumpled but engaging sort of hero wearing shades and driving his unmistakable 50's convertible. When Ray rings up the speaking clock and is told the world's about to end and then a famous Russian scientist steals his Oldsmobile, he's left in a daze. But when he switches on the Electric Lullaby machine, the nightmare really begins . . .

Z to A Know Your Body Backwards by Charlie Green
014090171X

Here it is at last! The book you've been waiting for ever since you spotted the very first spot or split that very first end. Everything from eyes to fingers; from healthy eating to using make-up; from what to wear to underwear and other unmentionables is discussed in detail by top fashion and beauty expert, Charlie Green. Working with fashion models in exotic locations all over the world, Charlie knows the beauty business backwards and major stars such as Kylie Minogue rely on her beauty tips and secrets to look their best. Now you can share those secrets. Know Your Body Backwards from Z to A today!

The Year I Was Born 1981   014090199X
The Year I Was Born 1982   0140902007
The Year I Was Born 1983   0140902015
The Year I Was Born 1984   0140902023
compiled by Sally Tagholm

These colourfully illustrated books will enable you to
discover all about the year of your birth and what makes it so
unique. The books are like diaries, and whichever you
choose, it gives a day-by-day picture of your year, with items
of information ranging from the national disaster to pieces of
idle gossip, from the tragic to the humorous. Packed full of
exciting, interesting and sometimes bizarre news items, this
wonderful series of books brings each special year to life.